For Kathleen and
Evi with love
V. F.
For Rob and Elaine
C. F.

ISBN 0-590-98778-X

Text copyright © 1991 by Vivian French.
Illustrations copyright © 1991 by Chris Fisher.
All rights reserved.
Published by Scholastic Inc., 555 Broadway, New York, NY 10012,
by arrangement with Candlewick Press.
SCHOLASTIC and associated logos are trademarks and/or registered
trademarks of Scholastic Inc.

12 11 10 9 8 7 6 5 4 3 2 1   8 9/9 0 1 2 3/0

Printed in the U.S.A.   24

First Scholastic printing, December 1998

This book was typeset in New Century Schoolbook and M Nimrod.
The pictures were done in watercolor.

Christmas Kitten

Vivian French

illustrated by
Chris Fisher

SCHOLASTIC INC.
New York Toronto London Auckland Sydney
Mexico City New Delhi Hong Kong

It was the day before Christmas and it was very cold.
A little black kitten was hungry and lonely.
"Meeeow," he said. "Meeeow."
"What a sweet little kitten," said a small girl. "I *do*
want a kitten—can we take him home, Dad?"

"I'm sure someone's waiting for him, Sophie,"
said her dad. "I'll bet he's going home for dinner,
just like us."
"Meeeow," said the kitten, meaning, "No, I'm not.
Please take me home with you." But Sophie
and her dad didn't understand and hurried away.

Some children were playing in a yard.
"Meeeow," said the kitten, running up to them.
"Meeeow."
"Cat," said a little girl, picking him up.

"Put him down, Rosie," said a big boy. "We're not allowed to pick up stray cats—not even at Christmas." Rosie put the kitten down.
"Bye, nice cat," she said.

A store had shiny holly for sale, with Christmas cakes and iced buns and sugar cookies piled up high. The hungry little kitten stood in the doorway.

"Meeeow," he said sadly. "Meeeow."
"No cats here," said a man, "not even a little one."
And he shooed the kitten away.

The little black kitten
jumped onto a windowsill.
It looked so warm and
cozy inside.
"Meeeow," he said
hopefully. "Meeeow."
A little old lady crossed
the room to see him.
"What a pity I have a
parakeet," she said.
"You're such a pretty
puss," and she drew the
curtains.

It was beginning to get dark. The little black kitten shivered. The wind was blowing harder, and more and more people were hurrying home, carrying bags of Christmas presents.

"Meeeow," said the kitten. "Meeeow."
But nobody heard him, and he had to run in and
out, this way and that, to avoid their hurrying feet.

BEWARE OF THE DOG

The kitten crept along the snowy pavement like a little black shadow.

"Meeeow," he said in a tiny tired voice. "Meeeow." He slipped in between the bars of a gate to look for a place to sleep.

"Woof! Woof!" A dog jumped out and the little kitten turned and fled as fast as he could.

The little black kitten was running so fast that
he didn't see the sleigh and reindeer in
the road. He bumped right into it and landed on
a pile of warm dry sacks.
He sighed, curled up, and went to sleep.

The kitten woke up with a start. Someone was talking in a cheerful rumbling voice. "Whatever shall I do? I need just one more present, but there's nothing left in my sacks." The kitten wriggled out to look. "Meeeow," he said. "Meeeow."

"What have we here?" said Santa Claus.
"Just the very thing."
The kitten held on tight. The sleigh
flew up, up in the air . . . and soon landed.

Santa Claus scooped up the kitten, slid down the
chimney . . .

. . . and tucked him into a small stocking hanging
at the end of a small bed. "Merry Christmas,
Sophie!" Santa Claus called and dashed off
and away.

The kitten wriggled out of the stocking and fell
to the floor with a bump. Sophie opened her eyes.
"What's that?" she said.
"Meeeow," said the kitten. "Meeeow."

"OH!" said Sophie. "OH!" She picked up the kitten
and hugged him. "It's *my* little black kitten.
It really is. Oh, little black kitten, will you stay
with me for ever and ever?"
"Meeeow," said the kitten. "Meeeow."
And he and Sophie curled up together to wait for
Christmas morning.